Postcards from Barney Bear

Hi, my name is Barney Bear.
I like to travel everywhere.

From the bottom of the ocean
To the hot desert sun.
Read my postcards one by one.

Greetings from the *coral reef*

Dear Mom & Dad,
    Under the sea is a fun place! I saw fish, crabs, sea stars, and clams. I like all the pretty colors. I wish you were here.

    Love,
        Barney

Mr. & Mrs. Bear
123 Forest Way
Denville, CO
    81945

Greetings from
The
RAIN FOREST

Dear Ted,
I am in the rain forest. There are so many trees that I can't see the sky!
I saw a sloth, a parrot, and lots of monkeys.
See you soon,
Barney

Ted E. Bear
53 Hidden Cove Dr.
Woodland, WI
53642

Greetings from THE DESERT

Dear Grandpa,
Hello from the desert! There are no trees here. Most of the animals come out at night. I found a snake for you.
Bye! Barney
P.S. Just kidding about the snake! But I did find a snake skin.

Mr. Bernard Bear
471 Meadow Rd.
Bear Country, CA
90145

6

Greetings from
ANTARCTICA

Dear Annie,
I am in Antarctica.
This is a very
cold place. I saw
emperor penguins.
They are fun to
watch. I am looking
for a blue whale or
a killer whale.
Your brother,
Barney

Annie Bear
123 Forest Way
Denville, CO
81945

1. Make blank postcards. Cut poster paper into 4" x 6" (10 x 15 cm) rectangles.

2. On one side of the postcard, draw a picture of a place anywhere in the world.

3. On the other side, use the postcard format. Write a message and an address. Add a stamp and send the postcard to a friend or family member.

Greetings from The MOUNTAINS

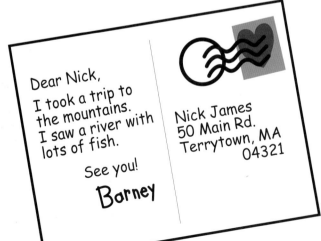

Dear Nick,
I took a trip to the mountains. I saw a river with lots of fish.

See you!
Barney

Nick James
50 Main Rd.
Terrytown, MA
04321